WARM UNDER A FOREIGN SUN

Kendall Brewer

CANDLEBREW PUBLISHING | AUSTIN, TX

Book Cover by Koby Hughes
First Edition, 2025

Paperback ISBN 979-8-9988289-3-5
Ebook ISBN 979-8-9988289-9-7

Library of Congress Control Number 2025911989

Candlebrew Publishing
Austin, TX
Email inquiries to candlebookbrewery@gmail.com
candlebrewpublishing.itch.io

brewer.neocities.org

Dedicated to all who have supported, educated, and welcomed me,

to Sarah Hoss for her time advising Rose State College's LGBTQ+ student organization, Spectrum Alliance,

and to my husband, Koby, for the sharing of our souls and lives together as one.

Readers are warned that some of the poems within contain sensitive subject matter that may be difficult to read. A blanket warning is made for dysphoria, misgendering, discrimination, genitalia, & erotic poetry.

An index in the back has been provided with specific content warnings; if there are topics that you suspect may strongly affect you, I encourage you to review this index.

Table of Contents

Foreword

I've been writing queer poetry just about as long as I've been writing poetry at all. As someone who also writes fiction, some of my poems ended up being written by, from the perspective of, or inspired by the queer characters I've created over the course of developing stories. I have queer friends who I write about, too, including my husband, who was so excited for the project that he made a cover for it the day I came up with a title and described the premise to him.

In the process of curating the manuscript for WUAFS, I realized very quickly that things would just be too...repetitive? if I only included poems about my own experiences, my own identity, particularly since the collection at its core is about the queer community as something warm and inclusive, rather than some miserable exile cast out from polite society. Therefore, not only did I feel it was critical to include a variety of identities and forms of love, I also realized it was critical to avoid drawing too much attention to my own personal experience. I am only one tree in a beautiful, vibrant forest, and my personal poems should not be interpreted by the readers as the main entree with optional, fictional side dishes.

I believe, too, in the importance of interpretation. As the writer, I am not G/d over what I've written. I own the copyright, sure, and I'm the one who strung the words together and arranged them into lines and stanzas, but poetry belongs more than anything to the reader. Therefore, it doesn't matter if a particular poem is from a particular perspective or inspired by a specific relationship dynamic; it matters how the poem made you feel, what parts of it resonate with you and what parts of it, too, that you reject.

Kendall

Humanity

There is no gender
for the deficiency you satisfy
in my body

There is no identity
for the nutrient rich soil
where I've established my roots

the sun might be alive

The sun might be alive
someone smarter than me once said
Because she regulates herself
shifting and scorching
until she finds herself
in a more comfortable position
Ready to watch her sweet silver dancer
spinning across her dark stage

the closet witnesses the bedroom

the naked lunar mass
heaving
silver shining liquid dribbling from the shores
temperate rainpour
on this night,
is it safe to worship?

A Small Town Wedding

Both of us queer
I am your plus one,
approved by the bride,
who's filled her audience
with lesbians and trannies
in various shades of the earth.

Our friends compliment
your handmade bolo tie,
my thrifted heels,
despite a few minutes ago
how a woman white as milk
asked how I know the groom
and when I said I know the bride
she hummed and looked away.

The drive down to this countryside
was full of confused stares,
from people in small towns,
from us, seeing MAGA trucks and
Don't Tread On Me flags

There's a pervasive sense of unease
as we await the reception,
despite us all being united,
wishing our hosts offered
non-alcoholic refreshments
under this Texan sunshine

Didn't we come here
to celebrate love?

a man & his dog | one

The burning flames of the sun
spill out and spread across the white sands of the desert
The wind in shuddering exhales sculpted these dunes
forming perfect curves and valleys

Boy Dessert

Soft dough,
A honey bread,
Sweet ichor dripping

I fit my mouth around it,
Splitting it in two,
Tasting the warm jam inside

Cake tender,
Soft against my lips,
Warm against my tongue

A tender berry,
Fat and ripe,
Fills my mouth,
As I tongue its soft flesh,
Its sugar coating my teeth
My hunger insatiable,
As I gorge myself on sweet delicacy

it's basically

My gender is something unspeakable
a forgotten tongue
the anonymous silhouette
in the driver's seat, behind headlights

That is to say,
unrecognizable

The Moon is a Woman

The moon is a woman
her beautiful glow and dimples
luminary spotlight upon her
spinning across her dark stage

Thunderstorm

Sunbeams filtering through tree branches
Golden light, glowing,
Warming me,
Knotted between my fingers,
Spread across white cotton

The low rumble of a thunderstorm builds,
A sound so sweet and raw,
Thrumming in my bones

Sweet rain washes over me,
Lightning cracking,
Crying out,
Sobbing,
My name between your lips

a man & his dog | two

The ocean rocks our boat to and fro
We tumble against each other,
the mass beneath us creaking with every rising wave
The storm crescendos until we are pressed together,
clutching, sobbing, trembling

every stag, a doe

you were born a woman
as practice for the head
you would one day give your wife

a slur manifesto

my cis friend
made an effort
to make queer characters
the only one nonbinary
was it/its
she argued that
the wiki page
said people use it
so she did too

i, tranny, might not be a fag
but my husband is
these words
refer to people
i love
and you must be fluent
in this love
before you can speak of it

transposing to a different key

you are a composer
a different note, every sound that comes out of you
i want to master the instrument of your body

a man & his dog | three

The sweetest delicacy is the honey stolen from the hive
Every gasp you breathe, inhaled
I rob the whimpers directly from your lips
in the white hot blaze that consumes us,
it is my name in your mouth, not his

Dam Overflown

A new river forms
rolling across pliant terrain
Streams like roots
dribbling down the skin
of your thighs

Prophecy Fulfilled

Like a fairytale,
my womb was a curse,
afflicted upon me at birth
my surgeon, the wise sage,
who freed me at last

i will pray for you

only love exists
in how i feel
building babel's tower
of my body

the feel of my husband's shoulders
his hairy legs
his new face
i bask in his radiance

only god could have
designed this, just
as only satan
could have created your hate

Warm Under A Foreign Sun

In a foreign land we live
They exile us grotesque few
Move closer, you who looks like me
I'm warmest next to you

In Defense of Gal Pals

When we first met
I thought I was in love with you
There's nothing erotic about it,
the way you colonized my mind

In my youth this meant
that I would have to see you naked,
kiss you goodnight,
love you the way they do on TV

My life is incomplete without you,
a seat at my table forever,
your dishes in my cupboard
I was sure I would have to love you

My professor told us about
Lincoln sharing a bed with another man
and showed us letters both sexes
would write to their "friends"

I saw us in those letters,
how badly I want to build
my life around you
You, who hears my every thought,
know my very soul like a twin

And he explained that friendship
previously had much more love
Friendship was more important
than even marriage, for the soul
and fear of being seen as queer
made love something "more than" friends

I am in love with you
with my entire heart
the way "just friends" used to love
so long ago

And now this means I can share your bed
I don't have to kiss you goodnight
but your favorite mug
still lives in my kitchen

Many women love each other
in a way thats more than just friends
But some of those women
writing letters long ago
surely must have been in love
the way that I am with you

T4T

Dark desire
Howling, healing,
language of kisses, of witnessing
Then, voice warm
Delirious death

left to our own devices

as your woman
i recognize
that there are vulgar delights
you can only share
with your fellow cannibals

none of us are sacred

charm my mad clay
incense in the air,
hoarse voices speaking in tongues
i circled her
no longer fingers
a few pants later
we're just meat
leaking disgusting rot
together

transgender is not a dirty word

between friends we talk about
our changed vaginas
no different than
discussing allergies
and which shoes to wear

we're not the ones
making everything filthy
get your mind out of the gutter
and try listening again

stop praising my continued survival

my love isnt brave
its just as vile as yours

I hear the way you talk about me

I'm not some creature in the zoo
inhuman
observed at a distance
I have a boring corporate job, too
salaried
paying your insurance claim
Has it ever occurred to you
closeminded
that we might be the same species?

how could we have known?

once, you let us die
you blamed our deaths on us
now you claim we are a new concept
invented in the modern era
to try to finish
our genocide

i often think about my septum ring

i often think about my septum ring
the soul of trans identity is gender euphoria
studies show conflicting opinions
about makeup in the workplace
in the original tale
cinderella's stepsisters mutilated their feet
trying to fit the glass slipper
and my retail manager once asked "do you even
know how to make yourself look good?"

my coworker wears her bonnet sometimes
on zoom calls
and another coworker's desktop background
is her wedding day
her husband in dreads and everyone smiling

professional presentation is a template
that only some people were made for
how do the rest of us get paid?

Condom Dispensers

The student council approved
The teacher senate agreed
My professor represented the cause

She was not allowed in
the meeting room
to present her case to the board
They left and passed her laughing
amongst themselves

The president told her
we don't want anyone
to think we have here
those kinds of people

Now we all know
here we instead have
your kind of people

it somehow hurts more

my mother
decorates for pride
and calls my husband
by his name

yet i am still somehow
her daughter

o virgin

O to imagine the taste
the honey warm and soft on your tongue
the nectar in your pliant mouth

O to see the dew
building on the clay of your skin
your body yielding as my fingers sink into you

O no mortal man should be as lucky, as blessed
to hear the hymns that left your mouth
the sweet noises that hung on your breath

O to be the one who filled you
to pour into the porcelain curves
until the cup ran over, overflowing

Instead I am the one who defiles you
I sink my teeth into you
I manhandle you as if you are cheap plastic
your hymns are primal, wordless howls

I leave stains on your porcelain
he handles you delicately,
but I know that clay requires kneading

His gentle fingers earn soft whimpers
with me you are an earthquake
roaring and trembling

His hands may have painted you,
glazed and shaped you first,
but I know you are mine

america's faulty foundation

why does queer have to be
vaginas fitting together
cock in holes that dont conceive

why cant queer be
the fact that i love you
and dont want to kiss you
and dont want to say i do

everyone talks like friendship
is less than
"more than friends"
ive loved someone
in the february way
and it was just as strong
as how i feel about you

i want to sleep in separate bedrooms
and i dont want your last name
but i want to spend forever with you

and even now someone will read this
and say "thats just love like normal"
and think im stupid,
dont know how to label what i feel

fuck you
if you think i dont know what love is
dont know the ravine between romance and friendship
ill pray your gay away
because thats what youre saying to me

a car packed full of female bodies

my friends are always
more vibrant than the cis men
that they choose to date

god bless america

im jewish
i see the holocaust everywhere
but especially
in the 80s

TDOR, TDOV, Tu B'shevat, Tisha B'av

I am not a tradition
is it yours?
You have made me other
It's just a performance for you today
I act in solemn honor

Seraphim

I am equally ashamed
that I could not protect you
from what you've become
and do not deserve
what you are now

moonbeam

the crescent of the moon
a sliver between your legs

is it like love?

is this meaning?
the way all things might have souls
the way all things might think and live
just like the sun
what if i told you,
that the somethingness that humans have
that makes us love and cry
what if it is not thought
but the desire to connect?
to communicate across oceans
to be read after we pass
the sun emits a sort of song
grand enough that other galaxies might hear
does she wish to sing to them?
or someone she already holds in her arms,
her beloved lunar wife

aphrodite & demeter

the eyes of the deity
swirls in orbit
sacred peach ripe
suffer in divine awe
the raw poetry of the dandelion

progress doesn't yet become us

isnt it beautiful?
--that is, we have become so loud
that within ourselves--
we can oppress each other

Acknowledgements

I have to credit everyone who's helped me along the way, both before and after publishing my first book of poetry, *You Don't Speak My Language*. Professor Kristin Hahn of Rose State College instilled in me my love for poetry, and taught me more than I ever could have deserved. My work is as strong as the foundation she laid for me as both a teacher and a mentor. Professor Sarah Hoss was the best ally and advisor our student organization could have ever asked for, and I'm so grateful for the support and enthusiasm she had for every idea we brought to her.

Thank you to all of my friends and the piece of the LGBTQ community that they provide for me, both online and in real life. Bekah, Buzz, Jack, Liam, Sean, and all my friends in The Hollow Tree. Thank you to all our ally friends who never fail to treat my husband and I with just as much dignity as they treat each other. Thank you to my autistic brother who affectionately calls my husband "brother-in-law" and has more ease understanding the idea of a queerplatonic marriage than many allistic adults.

A special, warm thank you to my husband, who has always been my number one confidante for all aspects of my identity, who I have always been able to be my authentic self around. You've made me bloom and become the best version of myself, something I can never truly put into words how grateful of I am. You're my twin, my star, the moon to my sun. I love you.

Author Bio

Kendall Brewer (they/them) is an LGBTQ poet who graduated from Rose State College with a degree in English and achieved further education at the University of Central Oklahoma. From 2019-2020 they served as President of The Spectrum Alliance, Rose State College's LGBTQ+ student organization. Their poems have been published in the annual literary journal Pegasus, and they are a James Axley Creative Writing Award finalist and an Axley Merit Award Winner. When they're not writing, they're out dancing at The Domain in Austin, TX, with their queerplatonic husband Koby, married Halloween 2023.

Warm Under A Foreign Sun is their second book of poetry. Find more at brewer.neocities.org

Content Warning Index

"Arbuckle Mountains" from
You Don't Speak My Language

I always told you
the only way I could leave
would be in a body bag

Instead, I left with you

***

You Don't Speak My Language explores the otherness of trauma, the isolation that comes with long-term neglect and suffering. When others can't relate to you, every conversation feels foreign, and the trauma can feel like a barrier, something unspeakable when you are amongst those who don't speak the language of tragedy. The poems within reflect the journey it takes to transform trauma from a non-verbal state, unspoken and silent, into a language that can be both learned for yourself and taught to others, achieving fluency and, more importantly, mastery of that which was an obstacle for so long.

Available in paperback and ebook. Purchase *You Don't Speak My Language* on Amazon, IngramSpark, and more. Scan the QR code or visit brewer.neocities.org/books#YDSML for all available retailers.